Sojourn™

FROM THE ASHES

D1489438

Publisher's Cataloging in Publication Data

Sojourn. Volume one : from the ashes / Writer: Ron Marz ; Penciler: Greg Land ; Inker: Drew Geraci ; Colorist: Caesar Rodriguez.

p. : ill. ; cm.

Spine title: Sojourn. 1 : from the ashes

ISBN: 1-931484-15-5

1. Fantasy fiction. 2. Graphic novels. 3. Mordath (Fictitious character) 4. Arwyn (Fictitious character) I. Marz, Ron. II. Land, Greg. III. Geraci, Drew. IV. Rodriguez, Caesar. V. Title: From the ashes VI. Title: Sojourn. 1 : from the ashes.

Sojourn™

FROM THE ASHES

Ron **MARZ**
WRITER

Greg **LAND**
PENCILER

Drew **GERACI**
INKER

Caesar **RODRIGUEZ**
COLORIST

Troy **PETERI** - LETTERER

COVER ART BY: Greg Land & Justin Ponsor

CrossGeneration Comics   **Oldsmar, Florida**

FROM THE ASHES

features Prequel
and Chapters 1 - 6
of the ongoing series
SOJOURN

Evil spread itself across the world of Quin.

The warlord Mordath put the Five Lands to the torch and the sword, conquering nearly all of Quin. But a mysterious warrior appeared and forged the victims of Mordath's tyranny into an army powerful enough to challenge him. Now Mordath is besieged in his castle...

...but any animal is at its most dangerous when cornered.

...BUT ITS APPETITE MUST ALWAYS BE SATED.

HOW MANY, MORDATH? HOW MANY OF US DO YOU THINK YOU CAN KILL BEFORE ONE OF US TAKES YOUR HEAD?

DON'T BOTHER REACHING FOR YOUR BLADE. YOU'LL BE DEAD BEFORE YOU EVER LAY HANDS ON—

UHHK!

FORGIVE ME FOR ALLOWING HIM TO GET SO NEAR, LORD.

ARE YOU WELL?

I LIVE, MAHK.

FOR NOW.

THE BATTLE?

POOR. THEY BREAK OUR LINES, SPILL OVER OUR WALLS. WE FIGHT VALIANTLY...

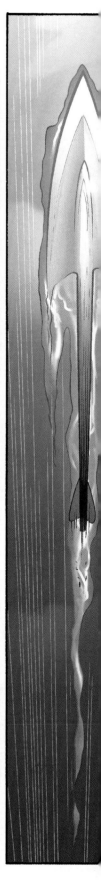

SPKK

NNFF!

NHH

⇒HH⇐ ⇒HH⇐

⇒HH⇐

⇒HH⇐

YOU'RE THE ONE WHO'S DONE THIS TO ME?

IF YOU ASK WHETHER I AM HE WHO HAS HELPED BRING ABOUT YOUR DEFEAT...

...YES.

SO THE MYSTERY IS JUST A MAN AFTER ALL. SOMEHOW I EXPECTED SOMEONE MORE...

...REGAL.

YOU COUNT YOUR VICTORY PREMATURELY. ARE YOU WILLING TO COME TAKE IT *PERSONALLY*?

SLAY HIM, LORD!

LET *US* CUT DOWN MORDATH!

HOLD.

ENOUGH BLOOD'S BEEN SPILLED.

ONCE YOU CAST A SHADOW ACROSS NEARLY ALL OF THE FIVE LANDS.

THAT IS NOW AT AN END.

IT'S AS IF YOU DID NOT *EXIST* BEFORE YOU MOVED AGAINST ME. WHERE DID YOU COME FROM?

I CAME TO THIS PLACE TO *REMOVE* MYSELF FROM STRIFE. TO BE AT *PEACE*. I HAD NO DESIRE TO INVOLVE MYSELF IN THIS CONFLICT...

...BUT *YOU* LEFT ME NO CHOICE. YOU FORCED ME TO DO THAT WHICH I FIND MOST REPUGNANT.

CHOOSE SIDES.

MY ARMY IS VICTORIOUS...

...WHILE YOURS IS NO MORE.

CONCLUDE THIS WHILE YOU YET LIVE.

...I WILL RETURN TO YOU.

I CAME TO YOUR AID BECAUSE I COULD NOT DO OTHERWISE.

BUT I HAVE NO DESIRE TO BECOME FURTHER EMBROILED IN THE AFFAIRS OF MEN.

SO I MUST BID YOU FAREWELL.

THEN LEAVE WITH OUR THANKS, LORD.

SHOULD YOU EVER THINK TO RECONSIDER, WE ARE YOUR SERVANTS.

WAIT. AYDEN...

...WHO ARE YOU? TRULY?

IN TRUTH I'VE BEEN MANY THINGS...

PLEASE...

HRLG!

AHH!

GHRRG

NHH

NHH

EVERYTHING'S ALL RIGHT. I WON'T LET THEM HURT YOU.

WHAT'S *YOUR* NAME?

I'M...

...MY NAME IS BRIA.

BRIA, THEN.

ARE YOU ALL RIGHT?

A LITTLE SCARED, BUT...

...I'M ALL RIGHT.

IS HE *YOURS?* WHAT'S HIS NAME?

THAT'S *KREEG.* I'VE HAD HIM SINCE HE WAS A PUPPY.

BRIA, LISTEN TO ME. IT'S VERY DANGEROUS TO BE OUT RIGHT NOW. THE TROLLS ARE ALL OVER THE CITY AND THEY'RE...

...THEY'RE DOING *BAD THINGS.*

IS THERE SOMEONE WHO'S SUPPOSED TO BE TAKING CARE OF YOU? YOUR PARENTS?

I WAS *WITH* MY MOMMY. WE WERE ON OUR WAY TO MEET MY DADDY SO WE COULD ALL LEAVE THE CITY.

AND THAT'S WHEN THE *TROLLS* FOUND US. THEY FOUND US AND THEN THEY...

...THEY *HURT* MY MOMMY.

BUT *I* GOT AWAY.

BRIA!

DADDY!

BRIA, THANK AYDEN YOU'RE *ALIVE!*

I NEVER THOUGHT I'D *SEE* YOU AGAIN!

WHAT ABOUT YOUR MOTHER. IS MOMMY *WITH* YOU?

NO, DADDY.

MOMMY'S GONE.

Shh, SWEETIE. IT'S GOING TO BE ALL RIGHT.

THERE WAS A TROLL WHO WAS GOING TO HURT *ME,* TOO...

...BUT THE LADY SAVED ME. THE LADY AND HER DOGGIE. *HIS* NAME IS KREEG.

When Mordath rose from the dead he gathered the troll armies to himself and led them across the Five Lands, just as he had three centuries before.

In his wake he left the burned husks of those who defied him. Once ultimate victory was within his grasp he returned to his fortress, bidding his troops exterminate the scattered opposition that remained.

Gerrindor was the last outpost to be conquered by Mordath's forces.

Nestled in a high valley of Erevin, it was a city known more for its arts than its ramparts.

Gerrindor's seclusion made it almost an afterthought. But even one city not under Mordath's heel was not to be tolerated.

The trolls fell upon it without warning...

...sweeping into the city like a tide.

I can't imagine she was prepared for what she found.

NO.

She hardly remembers any of it...

AHN!

...at least that's what she's told me.

UFF!

To her it's a disjointed series of images, lit by fire...

...and stained with blood.

I don't think saving **herself** ever occurred to her in any conscious way. The only thought in her mind...

I've never had what she had. So I've never **lost** what she had.

I can't say I truly know her, because she guards so much of herself. She keeps the world at arm's length.

But I think in some small way I've come to understand her. When everything you love is taken away from you...

...all that's left is hate.

And hate is at least something to hold on to when your whole life disappears...

...like smoke
into the air.

CHAPTER 2

NNH

NEERA.

HWFF?

NO, KREEG... IT'S OKAY. I WAS JUST—

I THINK I'VE RESTED LONG ENOUGH.

COME ON...

MNF

I'M SURE YOU UNDERSTAND WHY I CAN'T ALLOW THAT TO HAPPEN.

NNNN!

EVEN DEATH ITSELF COULDN'T PREVENT ME FROM DELIVERING MY RETRIBUTION TO THE FIVE LANDS.

NNNH!

AND NOTHING...

...NOTHING...

...WILL INTERFERE WITH MY ABSOLUTE GRIP UPON THIS WORLD.

WHAT'S *THAT* ABOUT?

THIS IS AS FAR AS YOU GO, KREEG. I HAVE TO DO SOMETHING AND I WON'T BE...

...I DON'T KNOW WHEN I'LL BE BACK. *YOU* CAN'T COME.

SO YOU... TAKE CARE OF YOURSELF, BOY.

I LOVE YOU.

WFF

KREEG, *NO.*

YOU'RE NOT SUPPOSED TO FOLLOW.

STAY, KREEG.

There are those who choose to believe Mordath is not **truly** Mordath...

...not the same man who united the troll clans and nearly conquered Quin more than three centuries ago.

Rather than accept he's risen from his tomb, they prefer to convince themselves the pale despot is some **other**...

...someone simply using Mordath's legend.

GRK

THUK

I know differently, of course. I've seen him with my own eyes.

But it doesn't matter what you believe. The reality is the same either way.

Mordath's rule is absolute.

Mordath is the most powerful being on all of Quin.

Powerful enough that only the mad would think themselves capable of destroying him.

GHLK!

HRR!

Of course, only the mad would seek to accomplish the deed...

"DINNER."

...by stealing into his fortress.

Alone.

My own visits to Mordath's fortress have never been undertaken willingly.

It's a vast edifice, as much a symbol of evil as the blood-red banners his troops carry into battle.

It rests upon the same plain in Middelyn once occupied by Mordath's original castle.

That one was torn down piece by piece following his death, the stones cast into the sea.

Upon his return Mordath had it rebuilt, and topped by a tower burning with a great flame fueled by his fiery power.

The beacon can be seen from great distances, a constant reminder of Mordath's rule.

WHO ARE—

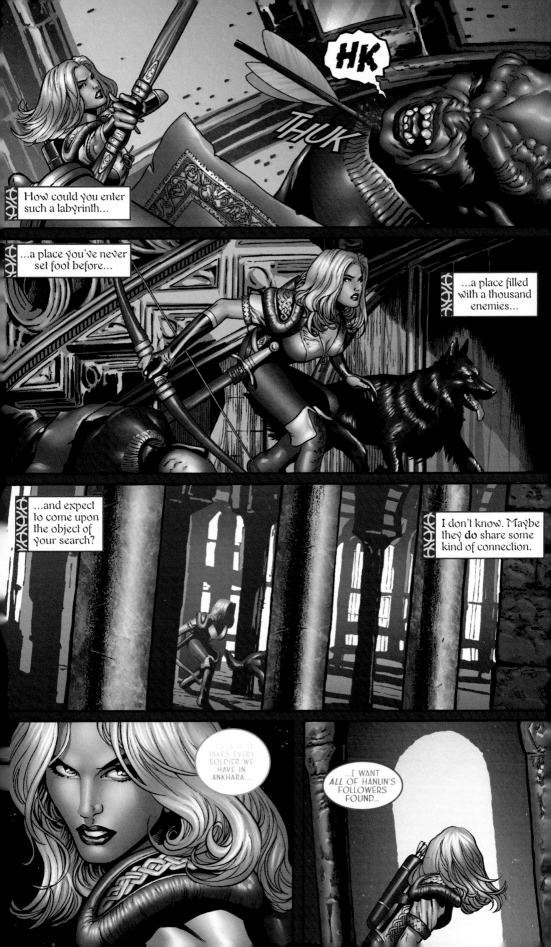

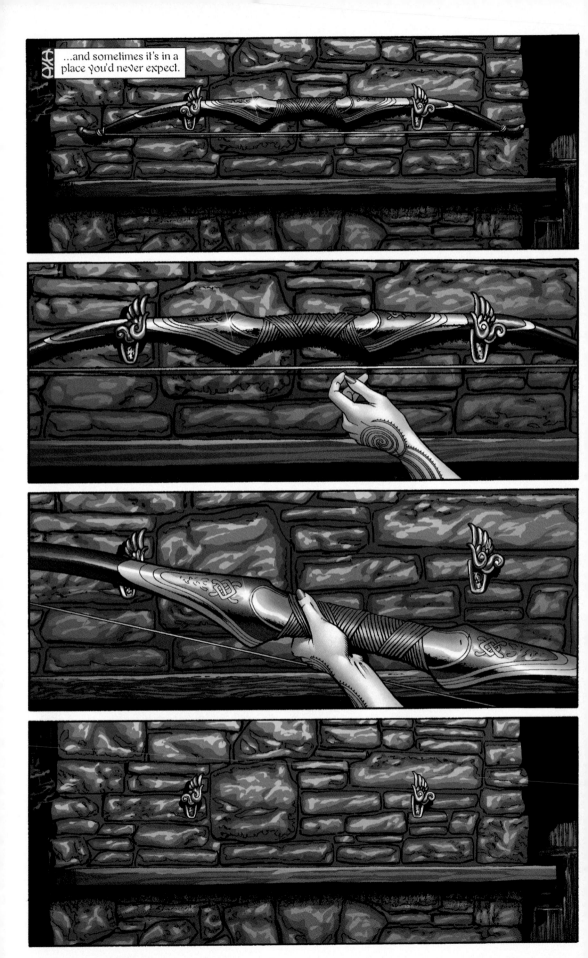

CHAPTER 3

She's a beautiful woman. Stunningly so.

HELLO?

And yet she acts as if the thought never crosses her mind, as if she's not even aware of it.

HELLO, CAN YOU HEAR ME?

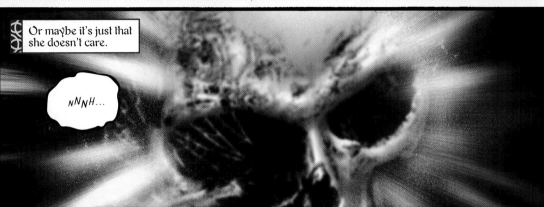

Or maybe it's just that she doesn't care.

NNNH...

...HNN?!

NO, NO, LOOK *THIS* WAY...

But it's impossible not to see it...

WHY HAVEN'T THEY KILLED ME? MORDATH SAID HE WANTED ME KILLED.

I'M NOT EVEN SURE WHY THEY HAVEN'T KILLED *ME*...

...BUT THE TROLLS TEND NOT TO BE TERRIBLY CHATTY.

I CAME HERE TO *KILL* MORDATH.

SHNK

SHNK

YOU WOULDN'T BE THE FIRST.

LISTEN, YANKING ON THOSE CHAINS ISN'T GOING TO DO YOU ANY GOOD, BUT I'VE GOT A—

HANG ON...

...WE'RE ABOUT TO HAVE COMPANY.

YOU'RE WONDERING, I SUPPOSE...

I SAID, "I'M SORRY." ABOUT YOUR FAMILY.

I CAN'T IMAGINE ANYTHING MORE TERRIBLE.

Oh...

...THANK YOU.

MY NAME IS *ARWYN*.

I LIVE IN GERRINDOR. *LIVED*.

WE HOPED THE CITY MIGHT BE SPARED BECAUSE IT WAS ON THE NORTHERN BORDER, AND THERE WAS NO OPEN REBELLION TO MORDATH'S RULE.

BUT MORDATH DOESN'T ALLOW *ANYTHING* TO ESCAPE HIS GRASP, DOES HE? SO THE TROLLS SWEPT INTO GERRINDOR.

I THINK I MIGHT BE THE ONLY SURVIVOR.

KREEG IS ALL I HAVE LEFT.

I'VE HAD HIM SINCE MY HUSBAND GAVE HIM TO ME AS A PUPPY.

WHY ARE *YOU* HERE?

USING ONE TOO MANY TROLLS FOR TARGET PRACTICE.

BUT I DON'T PLAN ON *STAYING* HERE.

WHAT DO YOU MEAN?

THIS. I TOOK IT OFF ONE OF THE DIMMER GUARDS...

...WHICH DOESN'T NARROW IT DOWN MUCH, I KNOW...

...BUT IT'S FAIRLY USELESS TO *ONE* PERSON. SEE? I CAN'T REACH THE OTHER MANACLE.

BUT WITH *TWO* PEOPLE...

KLAK

HERE. HURRY UP, THE TROLLS ARE LIABLE TO COME BACK AT ANY TIME.

KLAK

HUMAN! HOW DID YOU—

Ah

THE THINGS I DO...

NNF

...FOR SOMEBODY I JUST MET.

HHK!

GRGL!

ARWYN? DON'T TAKE THIS THE WRONG WAY, BUT...

...WHAT ARE YOU THINKING?!

NO OFFENSE...

I'M ENJOYING THIS *SO* MUCH MORE THAN BEING IN THE DUNGEON!

CAN'T GET MUCH BETTER, CAN IT?

CHASED THROUGH THE CASTLE OF AN UNDEAD EVIL TYRANT, A HORDE OF TROLLS AT MY HEELS, A DOG AND A MADWOMAN FOLLOWING ME...

...AND *SHE'S* GOT THE DAMN BOW.

COME ON, MAYBE THIS WAY...

...OR *NOT.*

HRAAAA

SHUKT

NOT *GOOD*, ARWYN! TROLLS IN FRONT OF US, TROLLS BEHIND US!

GYAA!

HOW IN AYDEN'S NAME DO WE GET *OUT* OF THIS PLACE?!

WE TRY *THERE!*

GRRFF

YOU'RE RIGHT... ...THIS *DOES* LOOK LIKE THE END.

There's something else.

I admit, up until then most women didn't hold my interest for much longer than it took to coax them out of their frocks.

But not Arwyn.

Equal parts sadness and rage is an intriguing combination.

NOWHERE LEFT TO RUN, SMOOTH SKINS!

THUK

LAST ARROW.

APPARENTLY *THIS* IS WHERE WE MAKE OUR STAND.

AT LEAST WE GOT TO ENJOY THE VIEW.

Meeting her changed my life.

I WANT THE GIRL.

Heh.

Maybe it's changed hers a little as well.

Huh?

Still, back then I was fairly certain the extent of our relationship would be dying together.

WHAT...

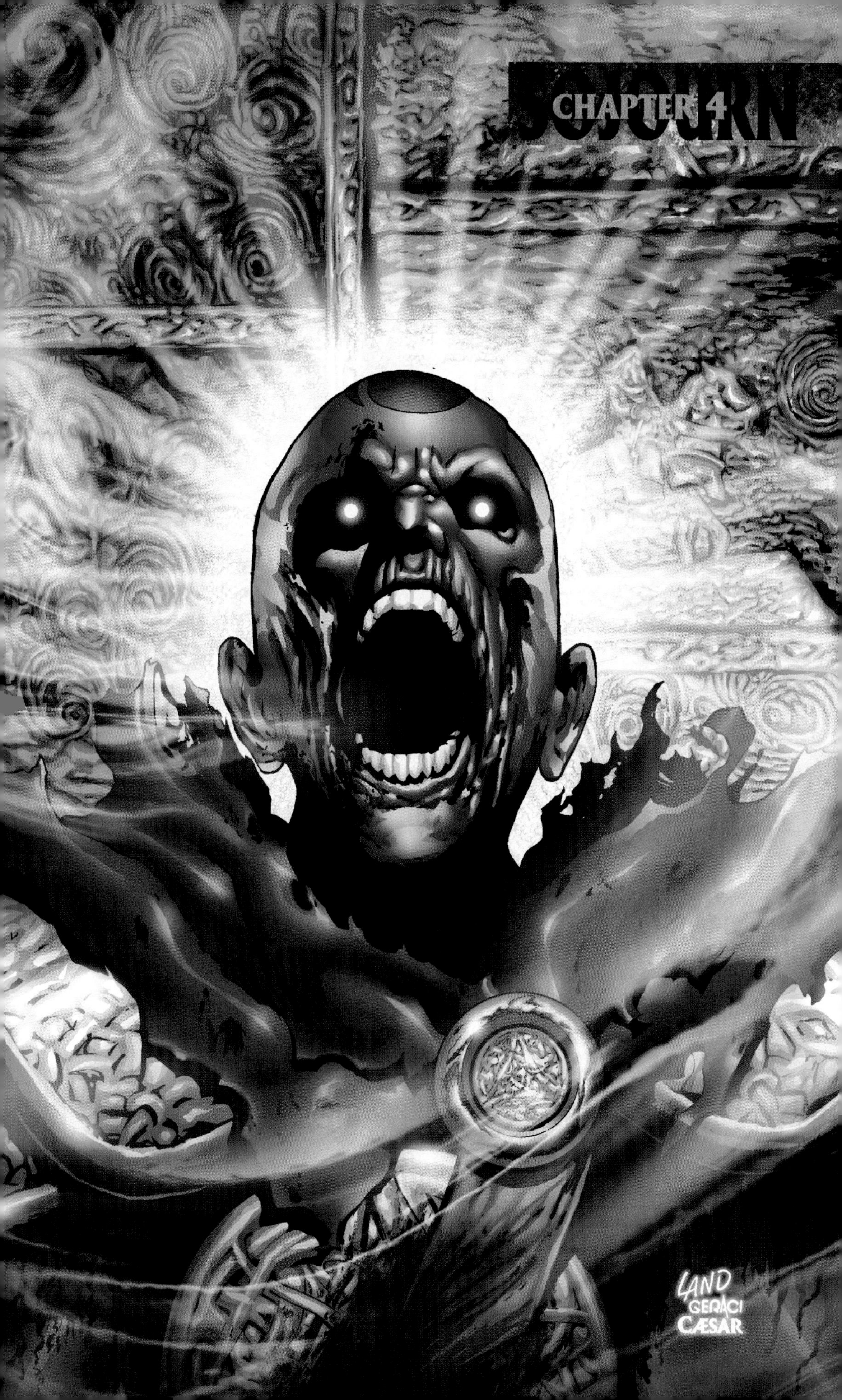
SOJOURN
CHAPTER 4
LAND
GERACI
CÆSAR

"...OUR WARRIORS AT THEIR HEELS. THEY'D SPENT THEIR LAST ARROW...

"...THEY WERE AT OUR MERCY, PREPARED TO MAKE A FINAL STAND.

"OUR WARRIORS ADVANCED WITH EVERY INTENTION OF DESTROYING THEM...

"...BUT HESITATED WHEN A *LIGHT* APPEARED BEHIND THE PRISONERS."

AS I SAID, LORD, THEY *DISAPPEARED.*

I'M SORRY.

DISAPPEARED. WITH THE AID OF SOME KIND OF *PHANTOM.*

THIS ARCHER...

...ARWYN...

...DO YOU UNDERSTAND WHO SHE IS TO ME?

SHE IS A *SURVIVOR.* SHE HAD THE AUDACITY TO COME HERE AND TRULY BELIEVE SHE COULD SLAY ME.

SHE *DEFIES* ME.

AND NOW SHE HAS SLIPPED THROUGH MY GRASP.

MY WILL IS UNCHALLENGED IN THE FIVE LANDS, SAVE FOR *THIS* WOMAN.

I WON'T ABIDE IT. SO YOU, BOHR...

...YOU WILL *FIND* HER.

TAKE AS MANY WARRIORS AS YOU NEED, KILL THE OTHERS WITH HER. BUT I WANT *HER* FOUND AND BROUGHT TO ME.

YES, LORD.

YOU KNOW THE PRICE OF FAILING ME, BOHR...

...DON'T FORCE ME TO EXACT IT FROM YOU.

IN OTHER WORDS, YOU WANT PAWNS.

WHOEVER YOU ARE, YOU CAN *DO* THINGS. THAT WE'RE STANDING HERE INSTEAD OF LYING DEAD AT THE TOP OF THAT TOWER IS PROOF OF IT.

BUT YOU'RE CHOOSING TO BECOME INVOLVED *NOW?* AFTER MORDATH HAS CONQUERED THE FIVE LANDS?

AFTER MY HUSBAND AND MY DAUGHTER WERE BUTCHERED?

SHE SAVED US, ARWYN. THAT HAS TO COUNT FOR SOMETHING.

THE LEAST WE OWE HER IS A CHANCE TO EXPLAIN HERSELF.

THERE'S A GREAT DEAL I *CAN'T* EXPLAIN TO YOU.

CAN'T OR *WON'T?*

ARWYN.

YOU SHOULD BE CONCERNING YOURSELF WITH *MORDATH...*

...NOT WITH ME.

EVERYONE KNOWS THE TALE OF HOW MORDATH *DIED...*

"...I CAN TELL YOU HOW HE CAME TO *LIVE AGAIN*.

"FOLLOWING HIS DEATH AT AYDEN'S HANDS, MORDATH WAS TO BE CAST INTO THE SEA, ALONG WITH THE RUBBLE OF HIS RAZED FORTRESS...

"...SO HIS CORPSE COULD TAINT NO PART OF THE FIVE LANDS.

"BUT BEFORE IT COULD BE ACCOMPLISHED, A SMALL FORCE OF TROLLS STOLE HIS BODY, EVENTUALLY SEALING IT WITHIN A SECRET TOMB IN THE MOUNTAINS OF GRINBOR.

"AND THERE IT STAYED FOR THREE HUNDRED YEARS, WITH ONLY DARKNESS AND SILENCE AS COMPANIONS.

"UNTIL A *FIGURE* APPEARED WITHIN THE TOMB, CONTEMPLATED THE DEAD TYRANT...

"BUT MORDATH WAS A CREATURE OF UTTERLY MALIGN INTENT.

"THE SHEER FORCE OF HIS SINISTER NATURE PERVERTED HIS SIGIL'S BALANCE...

"...TURNING ITS ENTIRETY AS CRIMSON AS THE BLOOD SPILLED BY HIS MARAUDING ARMIES.

"HE WAS WRENCHED BACK FROM THE VOID, HIS LIFE RETURNING JUST AS PAINFULLY AS IT WAS TAKEN...

"...A RESURRECTION AS VIOLENT AS HIS END."

"WHAT ROSE FROM THAT GRAVE WAS THE SAME MORDATH SLAIN BY AYDEN...

"...YET A MORDATH BITTERLY CHANGED, AND MADE INFINITELY MORE DANGEROUS.

"HE DIDN'T QUESTION THE METHOD OF HIS RETURN, NOR THE MOTIVE BEHIND IT. IT WAS ENOUGH TO LIVE AGAIN...

"...SO HE COULD WREAK HIS REVENGE UPON A WORLD THAT HAD SLIPPED HIS GRASP ONCE.

"BUT AS MORDATH PLOTTED HIS VENGEANCE, HE WAS UNAWARE THAT THE VERY WALLS OF HIS TOMB...

"...HELD THE KEYS TO HIS DESTRUCTION."

AND YOU EXPECT ME TO *BELIEVE* THAT...

...ON *YOUR* WORD ALONE?

A *"FIGURE"* BROUGHT MORDATH BACK FROM THE DEAD. IN A SEALED TOMB.

WITH A *TOUCH.*

YOU MUST THINK ME DULL-WITTED. HOW COULD YOU *POSSIBLY* BEGIN TO KNOW SUCH THINGS?

I *DO* KNOW...

...JUST AS I KNOW *YOU* WILL BE THE ONE WHO HERALDS MORDATH'S DEATH.

Oh, THIS IS WONDERFUL.

HOW DID I GET LUCKY ENOUGH TO BE STUCK WITH *TWO* MADWOMEN?

YOU'RE CRAZY... ...BOTH of you....

...IF YOU ACTUALLY BELIEVE YOU HAVE A PRAYER OF DESTROYING MORDATH. WE'VE GOT, WHAT, ONE SWORD BETWEEN THE THREE OF US?

YOU THINK THERE WERE A LOT OF TROLLS CHASING US THROUGH HIS CASTLE? HE HAS ARMIES OF THEM...

...WHICH IS WHY THE FIVE LANDS ARE COMPLETELY IN HIS CONTROL. WE WERE LUCKY TO ESCAPE WITH OUR LIVES, ARWYN...

...LET'S LEAVE IT AT THAT.

WE SHOULDN'T BE TALKING ABOUT DESTROYING MORDATH, WE SHOULD BE TALKING ABOUT GETTING AS FAR AWAY AS POSSIBLE.

A LOT FARTHER THAN THE RUINS OF ORELYN CASTLE.

I WATCHED MY CITY BURN. I FELT THE HEAT ON MY FACE AND I SWORE I'D KILL MORDATH. I'LL FIND A WAY TO DO IT...

...AND I DON'T NEED HELP FROM SOME MYSTERY WOMAN WHO SPEAKS IN RIDDLES OR A ONE-EYED SMART MOUTH WHO WANTS TO RUN THE OTHER WAY.

I DON'T NEED ANYONE.

KREEG...

...COME.

HWUFF

DON'T GIVE ME THAT LOOK, KREEG.

COME.

HE'S A SMART DOG. HE DOESN'T WANT YOU TO LEAVE.

I DON'T WANT YOU TO LEAVE, EITHER.

HERE...

CHAPTER 5

WHERE ARE THEY?

I SWEAR...

...I'M TELLING THE TRUTH.

THIS TASK WAS LAID BEFORE US BY LORD MORDATH HIMSELF.

WE CAME TO THIS DUNGHEAP OF A VILLAGE SEEKING HELP...

...AND YOU'VE BEEN NO HELP AT ALL!

GLRK!

WAIT!

PLEASE, DON'T KILL HIM!

GIVE ME A *REASON* NOT TO KILL HIM.

NNF

I SAW SOMETHING. EARLIER TONIGHT.

I WAS RETURNING FROM THE COUNTRYSIDE AND I SAW A LIGHT IN THE RUINS OF ORELYN CASTLE.

NONE OF *US* EVER GO THERE. EVERYONE SAYS THE RUINS ARE HAUNTED.

BUT THERE WAS A *LIGHT*. IT COULD HAVE BEEN A CAMPFIRE.

THAT'S ALL I KNOW. THAT'S ALL *ANYONE* KNOWS.

YOU'VE BEEN VERY ACCOMMODATING.

Hmf.

I WONDER HOW MUCH *MORE* ACCOMMODATING YOU CAN BE.

PLEASE, *DON'T...*

ENOUGH.

"...AND WE'LL SEE WHAT HIDES IN THESE RUINS."

IT'S *WHAT?*

AYDEN'S BOW.

AND NOW IT'S YOURS.

You could call Arwyn a lot of things.

DO YOU TAKE ME FOR A *FOOL?*

Gullible isn't one of them.

IF YOU CAN'T BE BOTHERED TO TELL US WHO YOU REALLY ARE AND WHAT YOU WANT, I CAN'T BE BOTHERED TO LISTEN.

I'VE TOLD YOU MY NAME IS NEVEN.

I'VE TOLD YOU I WANT MORDATH'S REIGN BROUGHT TO AN—

GRRRR

EASY, BOY.

SHUSH, KREEG. THE LAST THING WE NEED IS FOR YOU TO START BARKING AT SHADOWS.

I'VE REVEALED TO YOU ALL THAT I CAN, ARWYN. THERE ARE THINGS WHICH MUST REMAIN MINE ALONE TO KNOW, ASPECTS OF A LARGER TAPESTRY THAT DON'T CONCERN YOU.

MY DESIRE TO BRING ABOUT MORDATH'S DOWNFALL IS GENUINE. AND I *DID* SAVE YOUR LIVES.

IS IT SO HARD FOR YOU TO HAVE FAITH?

YES.

"SO MUCH BLOOD SPILLED IN OUDUBAI THAT NOT EVEN THE DESERT SANDS COULD ABSORB IT.

"THE CRYSTAL CITIES OF SKARNHIME SHATTERED AND MELTED.

"AND FINALLY MIDDELYN. FINALLY *GERRINDOR*.

"THIS TIME NO AYDEN RODE FORTH TO DRIVE MORDATH BACK. NO ONE APPEARED AND UNITED THE WARRIORS OF THE FIVE LANDS.

"THERE ARE NONE TO STAND AGAINST HIM, NO POWER CAPABLE OF MATCHING HIS.

"MORDATH *WILL* SMOTHER QUIN IN HIS GRASP. HE COULD EVEN BRING DESTRUCTION TO A MUCH *GRANDER* SCHEME..."

...UNLESS SOMEONE STOPS HIM.

AND YOU ACTUALLY BELIEVE GIVING ME THIS BOW WILL SOMEHOW BRING ABOUT MORDATH'S DOWNFALL?

OF COURSE.

HOW ELSE WILL YOU FIND THE FIVE FRAGMENTS AND BRING AYDEN BACK TO THE FIVE LANDS?

THAT'S WHAT THIS IS ABOUT? SENDING ME OFF ON A QUEST TO GATHER THE FIVE FRAGMENTS?

THE *ONLY* WAY TO DEFEAT MORDATH IS TO SUMMON AYDEN.

AYDEN LIVED THREE HUNDRED YEARS AGO! HE'S *DEAD!*

MORDATH *DIED* THREE HUNDRED YEARS AGO. HE'S ALIVE.

GRRRF

KREEG, I TOLD YOU TO BE *QUIET*.

THESE RUINS ARE SUPPOSED TO BE HAUNTED, RIGHT?

OLD KING WHATSISNAME?

HROOOWL

THERE'S DEFINITELY SOMETHING OUT THERE...

...BUT I DOUBT IT'S A GHOST.

Faith is a dangerous thing.

I DON'T SUPPOSE YOU BROUGHT ANY *ARROWS*.

Like believing the Five Fragments will truly summon Ayden back from wherever he went after slaying Mordath.

Or believing Ayden still exists **at all** three hundred years later.

Neven placed a quest before Arwyn and asked her to take it up on faith alone.

Like I said, dangerous thing.

Believe too little and you blind yourself to what's possible. Believe too much and you blind yourself to what's real.

HLLRG!

ABOUT TIME SOMEBODY HAS A BOW *I* CAN USE.

NNF

FWOK

THANKS.

HERE.

THANKS.

And it doesn't help that things are so often not what they seem.

DON'T *WASTE* ANY...

...I THINK WE'RE GOING TO NEED *ALL* OF THEM.

Who, for instance, would believe a one-eyed man...

...is really the greatest archer in all the Five Lands?

GFF!

THUK

AAGH!

THUK

I **did** say I've been called a lot of things.

YOU...

...YOU'RE **THAT** GARETH?

GARETH THE **BOWMAN?**

I'M LIKELY TO BE *GARETH THE DEAD* IF WE DON'T GET OUT OF HERE!

You know what faith really is? Faith is a sword.

It cuts both ways.

CHAPTER 6

...BUT SHE DIDN'T TAKE *US* ALONG!

I've gotten a lot more used to Neven – the "pale friend" in question – appearing and disappearing as she pleases.

Back then, I was a little less forgiving.

GRRAR

Neven's idea of **help** is sometimes a little murky.

Spiriting us away from Mordath's fortress? Helpful.

Handing Ayden's bow to Arwyn, a bow that apparently makes an arrow something more than a stick with a sharp point on it? Helpful.

Deserting us in the ruins of Orelyn Castle with trolls surrounding us? Not so much.

DOOM

COME ON, WHEN THAT *HITS* I THINK WE WANT TO BE SOMEWHERE ELSE!

Neven wanted someone to take up a quest to reunite the Five Fragments of Ayden's arrow and summon him back to the Five Lands.

And Ayden, of course, is supposed to destroy Mordath, just as he did three centuries ago.

For reasons that still aren't entirely clear to me, she chose Arwyn to take on the task.

BACK! GET BACK!

Neven picked a funny way of trying to convince her.

KWUMPF

IF THIS PLACE *IS* HAUNTED, THE GHOSTS ARE GONNA BE ANNOYED WITH YOU.

BY THE WAY, SOME *BOW* YOU'VE GOT THERE.

BUT...

...I MISSED HIM AND THEN...I DON'T UNDERSTAND HOW...

DON'T KNOW...

...AND RIGHT NOW I DON'T *CARE*. BUT IT LOOKS LIKE IT MIGHT'VE PROVIDED US WITH AN ESCAPE ROUTE.

DOWN *THERE?*

HOW DO WE KNOW THAT'S A WAY *OUT?* WE DON'T EVEN KNOW WHERE IT LEADS.

WELL, NOW THAT YOU MENTION IT...

...NO, WE *DON'T* KNOW WHERE IT LEADS. BUT IF WE STAY *HERE* I'VE GOT A PRETTY GOOD IDEA HOW THIS *ENDS.*

WHEN YOU PUT IT THAT WAY...

...KREEG, *FOLLOW!*

NOW WHAT? WHICH WAY DO WE GO?

TAKE YOUR PICK...

...*ANYWHERE* IS BETTER THAN HERE.

WHY DID YOU TELL ME NOT TO...

...oh.

DEAD END...

...ON *BOTH* ENDS NOW.

CAN'T GO FORWARD, CAN'T GO BACK.

YOU'RE THE ONE WITH THE MAGIC BOW. ANY SUGGESTIONS?

I HAVE NO IDEA *HOW* THE BOW DOES THAT, BUT MAYBE I COULD USE IT TO BLAST THROUGH THE RUBBLE.

WHICH MIGHT BRING THE WHOLE PLACE DOWN ON TOP OF—

HWUF

WHAT'VE YOU GOT, KREEG?

A *GRATE*, LEADING WHO KNOWS WHERE.

GOOD BOY. MAYBE WE'RE NOT *STUCK* AFTER ALL.

LOOKS LIKE SOME KIND OF DRAINAGE TUNNEL.

IT MUST HAVE BEEN USED AS A *RUNOFF* FOR THE CASTLE.

COME ON DOWN.

SMELLS AWFUL.

WAIT 'TIL YOU GET DOWN *HERE.*

DON'T COMPLAIN. AT LEAST IT'S BETTER THAN TROLL BREATH UP CLOSE.

SO WE'RE BACK TO "WHICH WAY DO WE GO?"

PICK A DIRECTION.

EITHER ONE'S A MUCH BETTER OPTION THAN ANY WE'VE GOT UP THERE.

ALL RIGHT...

...*THIS* WAY.

We slogged through the filth and the muck for I don't know **how** long.

Long enough that I would've traded my good eye for a gulp of fresh air.

FEELS LIKE WE'VE BEEN CRAWLING FOR *LEAGUES*.

IS THAT...

...IS THAT A *LIGHT* AHEAD FINALLY?

I DON'T KNOW, I CAN'T SEE MUCH OF ANYTHING BACK HERE.

NOT THAT I'M COMPLAINING ABOUT THE VIEW.

WE'RE DEFINITELY COMING TO THE END OF THIS THING.

DO YOU...

...*HEAR* SOMETHING?

LIKE A RUMBLE?

TELL ME WHAT YOU SEE. IS THERE A WAY OUT?

THERE'S A WAY OUT...

RRARF

THANK AYDEN.

YES, I'M GLAD TO SEE YOU TOO, BOY.

YOU'RE ALL I HAVE LEFT.

I THINK IT'S SAFE TO ASSUME WE HAVE THE TROLLS OFF OUR TRAIL, AT LEAST FOR A LITTLE WHILE.

EVEN IF THEY DID FIND A WAY TO FOLLOW US THROUGH THE RUNOFF, I SERIOUSLY DOUBT THEY'D BE CRAZY ENOUGH TO TRY THAT PLUNGE.

I STILL CAN'T QUITE BELIEVE WE WERE CRAZY ENOUGH.

SO WHAT NOW? HAVE YOU MADE A DECISION ABOUT WHAT NEVEN ASKED YOU TO DO?

I'M... NOT SURE.

I'M NOT SURE WHAT COMES NEXT.

THERE'S SOMEPLACE WE HAVE TO GO FIRST.

I've finally come to realize why.

DOES THAT MEAN YOU'RE READY TO TAKE UP THE TASK BEFORE YOU?

NEVEN.

THIS IS PRETTY MUCH *STANDARD* FOR YOU, ISN'T IT? POPPING UP OUT OF NOWHERE, THEN VANISHING WHEN YOU PLEASE.

WE COULD'VE USED A LITTLE *HELP* BACK AT ORELYN CASTLE, BUT APPARENTLY YOU HAD SOMEWHERE ELSE TO BE.

YOU'RE *HERE*, AREN'T YOU? YOU DIDN'T NEED ME.

THIS DOESN'T SERVE ANY PURPOSE, GARETH.

YOU WERE THE ONE WHO TOLD ME TO GIVE HER A CHANCE.

WILL YOU GIVE ME A CHANCE?

WHY ME? WHY DOES IT HAVE TO BE *ME*?

I CAN TELL YOU ONLY THAT THE QUEST FOR THE FIVE FRAGMENTS *MUST* FALL TO YOU. ALL WILL BE LOST UNLESS AYDEN RETURNS.

I WILL AID YOU WHEN NECESSARY, PROVIDE YOU WITH GUIDANCE...

...BUT THIS QUEST WILL BE *YOURS*, NOT MINE.

BECAUSE YOU ORCHESTRATE, YOU DON'T PARTICIPATE.

SO YOU'VE TOLD US ALREADY.

I'M NOT CONVINCED AYDEN STILL LIVES...

...I'M NOT SURE WHY *I* WAS CHOSEN RATHER THAN ANOTHER...

...AND I KNOW I DON'T LIKE BEING *FORCED* INTO THIS ROLE.

She's driven by a need for vengeance. But this quest also has become about searching for answers about herself.

Who is she now? And can anything hold meaning for her after what she's lost?

NEVEN?

WHERE DID—

GONE AGAIN. LIKE SMOKE.

I THINK THAT'S THE SORT OF THING WE SHOULD GET USED TO.

SO YOU'RE REALLY GOING TO DO THIS. DO YOU EVEN *BELIEVE* IN IT?

I BELIEVE THERE'S NO OTHER WAY OF DESTROYING MORDATH.

WHAT ABOUT *YOU*, GARETH THE BOWMAN? WHAT ARE YOU GOING TO DO?

I WAS THE ONE WHO DIDN'T WANT ANY PART OF THIS, REMEMBER?

BUT IF YOU'RE DETERMINED TO CARRY THIS THROUGH...

...I'M CERTAINLY NOT GOING TO LET YOU DO IT ALONE.

IF YOU DON'T MIND A ONE-EYED ARCHER TAGGING ALONG.

WELL...

...KREEG'S A LOT OF THINGS, BUT HE'S NOT A GREAT CONVERSATIONALIST.

I'D BE GLAD TO HAVE YOU.

I THINK IT'S *MY* TURN TO ASK. WHICH WAY DO WE GO?

She doesn't have the answers yet. Neither do I.

WHY DON'T WE JUST SEE WHERE IT TAKES US.

But I think we'll find them along the way.

THAT WAS A LONG TIME AGO, WHEN I STILL CLUNG TO AN ILLUSION OF IDEALISM.

BUT NO MORE.

IT *IS* WITHIN YOUR POWER TO DESTROY MORDATH.

YOU SWORE YOU'D RETURN IF THE WORLD NEEDED YOU. IF THE FIVE FRAGMENTS WERE REUNITED.

YOU *ARE* NEEDED.

NO ONE NEEDS ME.

THERE WAS A TIME I WAS STILL FOOLISH ENOUGH TO BELIEVE UNITY WAS POSSIBLE. NOW...

...I'M OLD AND WEARY. I FEAR *DISCORD* IS THE TRUE NATURE OF THINGS.

IS THAT WHY YOU STOLE MY *BOW?*

TO PIQUE MY INTEREST?

IN PART.

I GAVE THE BOW TO A WOMAN, *ARWYN*, WHO UNDERTAKES THE QUEST TO GATHER THE PIECES OF YOUR ARROW.

THERE'S A BIT OF *YOU* IN HER, I THINK. SHE TOO HAS LOST A GREAT DEAL...

...THOUGH *SHE* DID NOT TURN HER BACK ON THE WORLD.

WHO ARE YOU *TRULY?*

ONE WHO HAS AN INTEREST IN A GREAT MANY THINGS.

MYSTERIES NO LONGER INTRIGUE ME.

I WILL NOT BECOME INVOLVED.

I EXPECTED NOTHING DIFFERENT. WILL YOU AT LEAST *OBSERVE* ARWYN, THEN...

THEY CALL HIM
BigRed
SOJOURN Penciler Greg Land

Comics are a second career for Greg Land, who spent 10 years as a commercial artist before submitting his first sample pages to a comic publisher. After a short stint on one-shots and mini-series, Greg landed his first regular series with DC Comics' *Birds of Prey*, where he quickly gained notoriety for his cinematic layouts, beautiful female figures, and clean rendering style.

"Ever since grade school, I always wanted to draw comics. That was my goal, all the way through high school and college. I was always in the art classes and always excelled at artwork. I went to Indiana State University on a Talent Grant and received my degree in drawing and painting." Greg landed a professional art job while still in college, but he never lost his desire to draw comics.

Telling stories through pictures truly is a lifelong passion for Greg. "I remember when I was a little kid how I used to take comic books and cut them apart, cutting around the figures, and putting them on a masonite board that my grandpa gave me and create my own fight scenes."

Big Red's come a long way from that masonite board to laying out CrossGen's number one fantasy series, but he still employs collage to achieve the painfully precise compositions for which he's become known. Working from roughs, he'll rearrange figures and adjust backgrounds several times until everything is just so. Then Greg pastes up the page and lightboxes his own work, adding the rich detail that has become a trademark.

I spend time on the roughs, working out design problems so they don't pop up on me when I'm putting the figures down on the page. I work out facial expressions. What is the character doing in the story? The body — how is that relaying the thrust of the story? This all starts with rough thumbnails that go to tighter character sketches that get laid out on the page.

For this particular piece, the story called for Arwyn to have just plunged into a body of water. Basically she and Gareth escape the trolls through a sewage drain. She's going to be a little tired, totally wet, yet absolutely beautiful.

I started with a simple sketch to get a sensual pose of her coming out of the water that wasn't too over-the-top and yet showed her in the sensual way that's just part of her character. Once I captured the body language, I played around with the tilt of her head and the direction of her eyes. Then I sized everything on my rough layout page and cut and pasted my roughs to get the composition I was looking for. I used a lightbox to go to the final drawing.

For the cover of issue #6, I was going for a montage of images featuring Arwyn and Mordath. I wanted Arwyn in a pose that would show her athletic body and create a dynamic across the page. And then by using the large image of Mordath and the map background, we establish him as a large imposing figure.

Laying this out, I probably used seven different elements that I worked around on the layout page until the positioning was right. After I was happy with the composition, I lightboxed a copy of the layout onto the final paper.

These shots are all done for the purpose of catching the essence of the character for a particular need of the story. Everything is an experiment, because you do something in your rough and go back to the final and tweak it up. Make things a little more determined by furrowing an eyebrow or gritting up the teeth.

I'm constantly playing around with expressions in the sketches. You can try different things with the layouts. That's what they are. They're ways to work around and try different things on the paper.

For instance, look at the troll. You'll notice there's a section where I cut it and slid the bottom of the jaw down in order to make the growl of the troll even more dramatic than what it was originally.

My favorite expression to draw is "sultry."

Let's just say that whatever the subject matter is, I have a way I want to approach it. If it's Arwyn, I want it to be sleek, athletic — to me, Arwyn has the ideal female figure.

With this being the first SOJOURN trade paperback cover, I wanted to show all the main characters of the series. I like the montage method, so that's my starting point, building out from a full figure of Arwyn, who of course is the main character. Then I knew I wanted Mordath to loom over Arwyn and the other figures. Gareth and Neven were placed in the piece to balance the composition, so that the reader's eye will flow across the page.

The original thumbnail is only five inches tall. That turned into a layout page and then went to cut-and-paste collage method until I got everything positioned just right.

The trade cover was built around a fully rendered pencil drawing from me, as opposed to hard-line work that I submit to an inker. So this was about using tonal values to create shape and form. Justin Ponsor then added computer painting techniques to enhance the tonal drawing. We talked a lot about overall color scheme and atmospheric effects and then he went to town.

We were going more for an image that you might see with a movie poster, with dramatic lighting, and I feel that Justin did a very good job achieving that goal. Lighting creates a drama in itself, and Justin nailed it.

LAND

CROSSGEN COMICS

Graphic Novels

THE FIRST 1
Two Houses Divided $19.95   1-931484-04-X

THE FIRST 2
Magnificent Tension $19.95   1-931484-17-1

MYSTIC 1
Rite of Passage $19.95   1-931484-00-7

MYSTIC 2
The Demon Queen $19.95   1-931484-06-6

MERIDIAN 1
Flying Solo $19.95   1-931484-03-1

MERIDIAN 2
Going to Ground $19.95   1-931484-09-0

SCION 1
Conflict of Conscience $19.95   1-931484-02-3

SCION 2
Blood for Blood $19.95   1-931484-08-2

SIGIL 1
Mark of Power $19.95   1-931484-01-5

SIGIL 2
The Marked Man $19.95   1-931484-07-4

CRUX 1
Atlantis Rising $15.95   1-931484-14-7

SOJOURN 1
From the Ashes $19.95   1-931484-15-5

CROSSGEN ILLUSTRATED
Volume 1 $24.95   1-931484-05-8